This book belongs to

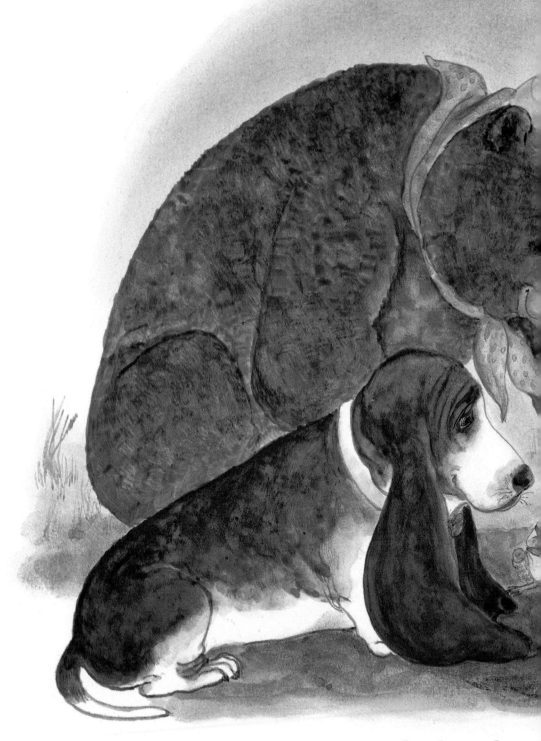

Animal

Friends

THE NOT-SO-FAST RABBIT

Animal Tales

A TALE ABOUT BEING SLOW

WRITTEN BY
CAROL B. KAPLAN

ILLUSTRATED BY
MIDGE QUENELL

Milliken Publishing Company – St. Louis, Missouri

Cover Design by Henning Design

Library of Congress Catalog Card Number: 87-62997
ISBN: 0-88335-079-3

Rodney Rabbit could hop
but not very fast.
In fact, Rodney was a very slow hopper.

When Rodney
and his brothers were young,
their mother said,
"I will name these fast little rabbits
Speedy, Quick, Jet, and Flick.

But this little rabbit...well,
I will name him Rodney."

As Rodney grew, he wished that he were fast like his brothers. "Don't worry, Rodney," Mother Rabbit told him. "You will find that being slow can bring good things."

Then she sang,

"Slowly, slowly, slowly go.
Many special things you'll know."

"What are the special things I'll know?"
wondered Rodney.
"What could be more special
than whizzing through the fields
with the other rabbits?"

Every day bright-eyed Rodney hopped
slowly from the forest to the farm.
On the way,
he stopped to listen to crickets,

watch birds,

and smell flowers.

He also stopped to chat
with Balaban Bear,

Wicker Basset,

and Frieda Frog.

And each day, his brothers raced by him.

"Come on! Come on!"
they shouted to Rodney one day.
"Get ready for the Great Rabbit Race.
Every rabbit should join the race!"

Rodney knew he was a slow hopper,
but he was a good sport.
He decided to join the race.

Balaban Bear
explained the rules to the rabbits.
"The race starts here in the forest.
You must hop to the farm
and shake paws with Wicker Basset.

Then you must hop back here.
The first rabbit back is the winner.
You may use any path you wish."

Rodney hopped slowly to the farm.
There he shook paws with Wicker
and began hopping back to the forest.

When he reached the finish line,
nobody was there except Balaban.
Balaban was jumping with excitement.

11

"Where are the other rabbits?"
Rodney asked.
"Have they gone home?"

"They aren't back yet, Rodney,"
said Balaban. "You are the winner!
My friend Rodney is the winner.
Hurray!"

Balaban lifted surprised Rodney
and gave him a bear hug.

"Well, I crossed the pond on a fallen tree.

I went under the hill in a hidden tunnel.

And I went through the fence
in a secret hole."

The rabbits were amazed
that Rodney knew these special shortcuts.

"Rodney knows a lot of special things,"
said Balaban.
"He hops slowly,
so he notices things that you don't.
He is quite a rabbit."

The rabbits
clapped and cheered for Rodney.
Then they went home.

Rodney started to hop home.
He thought about his mother's song.
"Were the secret shortcuts the special
things he would know?"

He stopped to listen
to the gurgling creek.

He watched a spider
spin her web.

He stopped
to taste a bit of clover.

And he softly touched
a feathery fern.

And Rodney thought,
"These are the special things!
By going slowly, I have learned about
many, many wonderful things."

21

He rested by the feathery fern
and sang his mother's song,

"Slowly, slowly, slowly go.
Many special things you'll know."

THE END

Mother Rabbit's Song

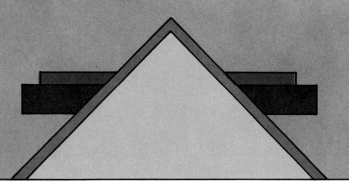

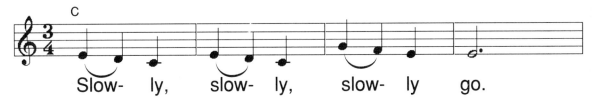

Slow- ly, slow- ly, slow- ly go.

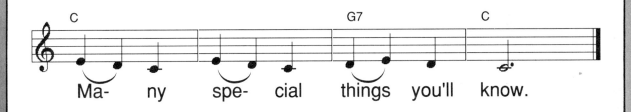

Ma- ny spe- cial things you'll know.

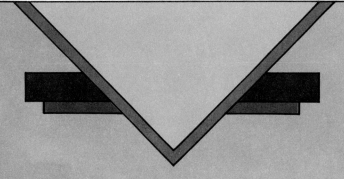